LACROSSE LEGEND

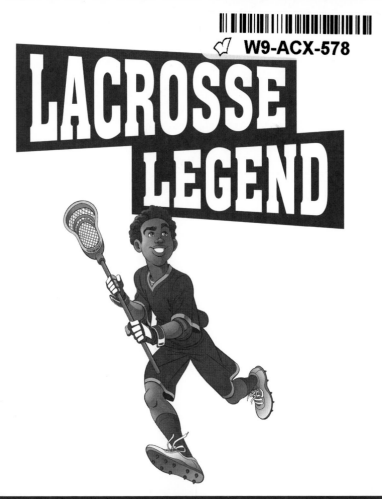

BY JAKE MADDOX

Text by Shawn Pryor
Illustrated by Pulsar Studio
(Beehive)

STONE ARCH BOOKS
a capstone imprint

W9-ACX-578

JPF
Maddox

Jake Maddox is published by Stone Arch Books, an imprint of Capstone.
1710 Roe Crest Drive
North Mankato, Minnesota 56003
www.capstonepub.com

Copyright © 2021 by Capstone. All rights reserved. No part of this publication may be reproduced in whole or in part, or stored in a retrieval system, or transmitted in any form or by any means, electronic, mechanical, photocopying, recording, or otherwise, without written permission of the publisher.

Library of Congress Cataloging-in-Publication Data is available on the Library of Congress website.

ISBN: 978-1-4965-9704-5 (library binding)
ISBN: 978-1-4965-9920-9 (paperback)
ISBN: 978-1-4965-9755-7 (eBook PDF)

Summary: Eager to follow in his father's footsteps, Ramon Hill wants nothing more than to be a starting attacker on his lacrosse team. Even though he's just a sixth grader, he makes the eighth-grade team, but he's stuck on the bench most of the time. At last he gets his chance to start, but there's a catch—he's asked to play midfield. Will Ramon be able to master his new position, or will he let his team and himself down?

Designer: Elyse White

Printed and bound in the USA.
PA117

TABLE OF CONTENTS

CHAPTER 1

WAITING FOR A CHANCE

The Centercreek Storm led the Allenburg Astros 10–3 with three minutes left in the game. Ramon Hill eagerly sat at the end of the bench and waited for his name to be called for Centercreek.

"Jax, go in for Bryce!" yelled Coach Yen. Ramon let out a sigh of disappointment as he watched Jax get up from the bench and run out to the field.

"Hey, rookie!" yelled Jax. "If you don't want to wait your turn, you can go play with the sixth graders!"

"I know, Jax. I know." Ramon muttered.

Ramon was the first sixth grader since his father to make the Centercreek middle-school eighth-grade lacrosse team. Now all he wanted was to show everyone on the field how good he is.

His father, Victor, was a great lacrosse player. He was a standout attacker from middle school through high school and even played professionally for a few years.

Ramon had only seen three minutes' worth of playing time all season. While on the bench, he studied every play taking place on the field. He was absorbing as much as he could so he would be ready when the coach called his number.

This game is over anyway, he told himself. *I want to play when it means something.*

Moments later, Bryce Craft, an eighth grader and captain for the Storm, sat next to him.

"Okay, Ramon, tell me what you saw today," Bryce said.

Ramon took a deep breath and exhaled. "Their midfielders are very slow, so it was pretty easy for us to deal with them. Their goalie jumps if you fake taking a shot, which leaves him open for easy goals. Their defenders are very tough. We still need to do a better job passing the ball or we're going to turn the ball over, especially when we play good teams."

Bryce looked surprised. "Wow, I didn't expect you to keep up with everything. Most of the guys on the team can barely focus on anything for five seconds, let alone the whole game."

"Well, it's not like I have much to do during the games," Ramon said sadly. He turned his head and saw his parents in the stands smile and wave at him.

"I know how much it stinks to not play," Bryce said. "We all know the pressure you carry from your dad being a legend for our school. But trust me, your time will come. It's rare when a sixth grader makes the team."

"I know. I just have to be patient," Ramon said as he looked at the game clock and watched the time slowly run down.

CHAPTER 2

IMPRESSING THE COACH

The following week, the Centercreek team was holding practice.

Coach Yen blew his whistle. *PHWEET!* "All right, time to scrimmage!" he yelled.

Ramon was excited. He looked forward to scrimmages. They were yet another chance to show everyone his skills. Until he started playing in the games, scrimmaging was his *best* chance.

He thought, *Maybe today is the day I finally show Coach Yen that I'm worthy of some playing time.*

The starters lined up on the field while the backup players took their positions as the opposing team. Ramon went to his left wing attacker position. He was eager for the scrimmage to begin.

Ramon's team won the face-off, and his midfielder passed him the ball.

"You're not going to get an easy goal on us, sixth grader!" Jax yelled.

He was on Ramon's heels, trying to create a turnover.

But Ramon was too fast for Jax, faking him and quickly passing the ball to Dexter who took an overhand shot to score a goal.

"I don't have to score a goal when I can set up others to do it!" Ramon called. He wasn't going to let the older boy intimidate him.

"You got lucky," blurted Jax. "You were scared to go against me and got a lucky assist."

"If you say so," Ramon replied.

Ramon continued to show his skills during the game, impressing most of the team.

With the scrimmage over, Coach Yen brought the team together. "That was a great scrimmage," he told the boys. "Even though the starters won, you backup players stuck right with them. That's what I like to see in my team."

"Starters are supposed to win," Jax responded loudly. "There's a reason why the nonstarters sit the bench!"

Ramon rolled his eyes. *Does he ever give it a rest?* he wondered.

"Ease up, Jax," Bryce said.

Coach Yen cleared his throat before continuing.

"As I was saying, even though the starters won the scrimmage, I saw a lot of positive things from our nonstarters today. I saw lots of crisp passing, solid defense, and setting up others to make plays. You even made the starters sweat." He seemed to look Ramon in the eye for a moment and added, "Nice job."

The team clapped as Coach Yen continued. "I'm sure you all have noticed that one of our starting midfielders, Jeff, wasn't at practice today."

"Yeah, where was he anyhow?" asked Bryce.

"His father landed a new job out of town, so he's going to be transferring to another school," Coach Yen explained. "We're going to have to make some adjustments before our game next week against Kirkland City. For now, let's call it a day. See you all tomorrow."

With practice over, the team broke out of their huddle and headed their separate ways. Ramon began to pack his duffel bag when Coach Yen called his name.

"Can I talk to you in my office?" Coach asked.

CHAPTER 3

THE OPPORTUNITY

Ramon followed Coach Yen out of the locker room. *I wonder what Coach wants,* Ramon thought. *Did I do something to annoy him or the team? Am I being demoted to the sixth-grade team?*

Sweating even more than during practice, Ramon entered Coach's office and sat down. Coach Yen closed the door behind him and then had a seat at his desk.

"Coach, I wasn't trying to show off during the scrimmage today," Ramon nervously said.

He was so worried that Coach was going to lecture him. He continued, "It's just that Jax gets under my skin sometimes and I wanted to show him that I deserve to be on the team."

Coach Yen smiled. "Relax. You're not in any trouble. In fact, I like that you continue to challenge your teammates on the field at every practice."

"That's good to know," Ramon said. He let out a sigh of relief and wondered, *So why am I here?*

"Your teammates are going to give you grief because of your age and grade. They'll also test you because of your last name and what it means around here. You've taken it in stride, though." Coach Yen said. "And that can be tough to do."

"Thanks, Coach," replied Ramon. "I appreciate it."

"As you heard me say before, Jeff is no longer on the team. That leaves us down a starting wing midfielder," said Coach.

Ramon replied, "Yep, he leaves a hole on the team, for sure."

"Well, after today's scrimmage, I was wondering if you'd like to take Jeff's place and start next week against Kirkland," said Coach. "I think you would be great at midfielder."

Ramon looked on in shock. "You want me to start next week? But, I've never been a midfielder before! I've played the attacker position my entire life."

"I know, but during the scrimmage today your passing skills and speed were impressive, and we need that badly in our midfielders. There will still be chances to possibly score a goal. But your attention will be focused on both sides of the field instead of one," Coach Yen said.

Ramon was unsure of what to do. He wanted to follow in his father's footsteps and be just like him. But that meant he might have to wait until next season to get a chance to start as an attacker.

However, if he switched positions, he could start right away. It was certainly tempting.

Still, Ramon wondered, *Will Dad be disappointed if I switch positions?*

"Think it over this weekend and talk to your parents about it," said Coach Yen. "I played alongside your Dad for a year during our college days, so I know what he and the position you play means to you. I'm sure you don't want to give up his old position too quickly."

"No, sir," Ramon admitted.

"I figured as much," said Coach. "So talk it over with them, and give me a call."

"Okay, Coach," Ramon said nervously. "I'll be in touch. I promise."

Ramon left the office wondering what to do. *You wanted a chance to play, and now you've got one. But will Dad be disappointed that you're not an attacker?*

CHAPTER 4

THE DECISION

Ramon was having dinner with his parents at Justin's Pizza Arcade. Ramon was picking the mushrooms off of his slice of pizza as his parents looked at him.

"Ramon, is there something wrong? You normally like mushrooms," his mother said.

Ramon was nervous to tell his parents the news. "Well . . ."

"You know that you can talk to us," his mother replied.

Ramon's father chimed in. "Is someone giving you trouble at school? Is someone on the team giving you a hard time? I can talk to Coach Yen if you need me to."

"No, everything's fine," Ramon said. "I had a meeting with Coach after practice today."

Both of his parents replied at the same time. "About what?"

Ramon took a deep breath and exhaled. "Coach wants to put me in the starting lineup in our next game against Kirkland City."

Ramon's parents' faces lit up with joy. "That's fantastic!" his mother said.

"I knew all your hard work would pay off, son!" his father said, ruffling Ramon's hair.

"Okay, okay, cut it out!" Ramon said, laughing and trying to get his father to stop. "There is one catch, though. I can start if I switch to the wing midfielder position."

His parents gave a brief pause, and then his mother asked, "How do you feel about it?"

"I really want to play. I also feel that I can make a difference and help our team win," Ramon said. He then looked at his father. "It's just that I've been an attacker all my life. If I make this move, am I letting you down because I'm not following in your footsteps? I just want to make both of you proud."

Ramon's father had a surprised look on his face. "Son, play the game for you and your team, not for me and your mother. We would support you no matter what you do. I know that you'll make the transition to midfielder just fine. Go for it."

Ramon let out a sigh of relief and smiled. "Thank you Mom and Dad. I'll call Coach Yen tomorrow and let him know."

CHAPTER 5

NEW POSITION

A few days later after school, the team returned to practice. Ramon was on the field stretching with his teammates.

Jax walked over to Ramon. "Listen kid, don't get a big head because Coach gave you a starting spot. There's a lot of us that aren't happy about it. If I had my way, you wouldn't even be on our team."

"Coach didn't give me anything! I earned this spot!" Ramon answered defensively. "You should use that attitude of yours against our opponents, not me."

"Whatever," Jax muttered, walking away.

Coach Yen blew his whistle. *PHWEET!* "Let's get to work!"

Practice began with Ramon playing in his new starting position. Within minutes, Ramon adjusted his offensive playing style. Then he worked on his assists and setting up fellow teammates to score.

Throughout the scrimmage, the players weren't taking it easy on Ramon. They bumped, shoved, and pushed him around throughout the game. He hung in there the best he could.

However, there was one minor issue that Ramon had while playing defense as a midfielder.

Coach Yen yelled and pointed to Ramon's position on the field, "Offsides! Ramon, when we're on defense and shift to offense you have to move fast!"

He continued to explain, "If you're still on the defensive side of the field while we're playing offense we're going to get hit with a penalty. That puts us a player down and gives the other team an advantage."

"Come on, get it in gear!" Jax yelled.

Coach Yen blew his whistle again. *PHWEET!* "That's enough for today. I don't have to remind you that the last three games of the season are crucial for us, but I will. If we win two of our last three games, we're playoff bound. See you tomorrow."

The team began to head to the locker room as Ramon stayed on the field. He took off his helmet. His hair was drenched with sweat.

"You did a good job out there today," Bryce said, putting his hand on Ramon's shoulder. "Don't let Jax or anyone else on this team get to you. Keep your head up. We need you on Friday."

"Thanks, Bryce," Ramon said. "I appreciate you saying that."

"We're a team, from the first player to last," Bryce said. "And I know when this week's worth of practices are done, you'll be ready."

Ramon smiled. He was thankful for the support from the team captain. He was going to play his best in his first start against Kirkland City.

CHAPTER 6

RAMON'S BIG START

It was finally game time for the Centercreek Storm. The starters took to the field as did the Kirkland City team. Ramon took a deep breath and lined up in his wing midfielder position.

Jax was ready for the face-off. He got into position in the center of the field. "Let's go Storm! Get ready!"

The referee blew the whistle. Jax quickly used his lacrosse stick to gain possession of the ball for the Storm.

He passed the ball to Ramon who ran upfield toward the opposing goalie.

Ramon quickly raised his stick, as if he was going to take a shot. Seeing Bryce in a proper scoring position, he passed the ball to Bryce who made an easy goal.

"Nice pass, Ramon! Way to go!" Coach Yen yelled.

Ramon gave Bryce a high five. "I got lucky on that one!" he said.

"We scored! That's all that matters," Bryce said. "Nice job!"

The first half continued with the Storm leading 8–2. Ramon had a few defensive steals and made three additional assists that led to goals. *Wow, this is going better than I thought,* he told himself.

As the second half began, their opponents started to play more aggressively and quickly tied the game.

Ramon was playing defense when Jax made a steal and they began to transition to offense. But there was an opposing player that got into Ramon's ear.

"You're not that good. The only reason you're on the team is because of your dad," the Kirkland player said.

"What did you say?" Ramon yelled.

The referee blew her whistle. *PHWEET!* "Offsides. Number seven. Centercreek! Thirty-second penalty."

Ramon turned to the referee, stunned. For being offsides, his team would now be down a player. He walked over to the bench, disappointed. "You have to stay focused, Ramon!" Coach Yen yelled.

"We're at a disadvantage thanks to the sixth grader," Jax screamed on the field. "Step it up, everybody!"

Ramon put his head down. Those thirty seconds felt like an eternity. All he wanted to do now was get back in the game and make up for his mistake.

With only five penalty seconds left, Kirkland City managed to score a goal, putting them in the lead.

Ramon heard the grumbles from some of his teammates as he ran back on the field for the face-off.

"Don't blow it for us," yelled Jax. "We don't have time to babysit you."

Ramon tried to keep the negative remarks out of his head.

"It's okay, Ramon! Shake it off and get your head back in the game!" said Bryce.

Ramon nodded in agreement as the referee blew the whistle and the Storm won the face-off.

While playing offense, Ramon was trying to get open for a pass and keep the defense on its toes. Catching a pass from Bryce, Ramon was elbowed by the same opposing player who caused him to get penalized earlier.

"Ow!" yelled Ramon, while making a pass to Jax.

"What's the matter kid, not tough enough to play? Do you need a diaper?" the Kirkland player said.

Ramon did his best to block him out as he continued to play. When the referees weren't looking, he was elbowed again. "Hey! Cut it out, man!" Ramon said.

"You're such a crybaby. Do you need your dad to come out here and give you a hug?" the opposing player said. "He's so overrated, and you're just a joke like he is."

Ramon had enough and slammed the opposing player to the ground.

"You don't talk about my father like that! Ever!" he yelled.

Another referee blew a whistle. *PHWEET!* "Personal foul. Number seven. Centercreek!"

Ramon ran over to the referee, trying to plead his case. "You don't understand. He was playing dirty and said awful things about my father and—"

The referee blew the whistle again. *PHWEET!* "Major foul. Number seven. Centercreek! No arguing with the referees! You're out for the rest of the game!"

CHAPTER 7

A MAJOR LETDOWN

Ramon waited alone in the locker room, in silence. In his entire time playing lacrosse, he had never had a penalty or foul called on him.

He caused his team to be a player down for the rest of the game. That left the Storm at a major disadvantage. *I can't believe I lost my head like that. I let Coach and the team down.*

The final buzzer sounded as the announcer over the PA system said, "Tonight's final, Kirkland City 15, Centercreek 11."

Ramon put his head down in shame as the team and Coach entered.

"And here's the reason why we lost tonight," said Jax, pointing at Ramon. "I knew it was a bad idea to let you play!"

"You screwed up big time!" said another teammate.

"Coach, demote him!" another player hollered.

Coach Yen put his hands up and said, "Everybody calm down. Tonight didn't go the way we wanted."

"Yeah, and he's to blame!" Jax shouted, pointing at Ramon.

"Look guys, Coach, I'm sorry," Ramon said. "I didn't mean to . . . That guy said things that . . . And I just . . ."

Ramon couldn't finish his sentence, and put his head in his hands. He was so disappointed in himself.

Bryce moved to calm down the team. "All right guys, enough is enough. Yes, Ramon made a mistake that cost us the game. But let's not act like we never made mistakes when we first joined this team."

The players began to quiet down. Bryce continued. "Jax, remember when you started your first game? I sure do. You tackled the goalie because you were mad that he blocked your goal attempt!"

Jax became very quiet and the other players began to hide their faces as Bryce went on.

"Remember last year when Robbie got the ball stolen from him fifteen times in one game? And that happened after the coach and all of us taught him how to protect the ball."

Robbie kept his head down and shrugged his shoulders.

Bryce continued, "Or how about last year's playoff game when Benson was going to score the tying goal with five seconds left on the clock and Luke accidentally ran into him and we lost. Did we constantly beat up on any of those guys?"

The team let out a somber "No."

Bryce walked over to Ramon. "The only way we can get better as a team is to help each other and build each other up. Before he got thrown out, Ramon made some great contributions on the field. We can't deny that. He's done everything we and the Coach have asked of him. He knows he messed up. Let's not make things worse and instead let's be better teammates."

Coach Yen stepped in. "We've got to win our next two games to make the playoffs. Can we make it happen? Can we get it done together?"

The team yelled all together, "YES!"

Ramon was thankful for Bryce speaking up for him. But after tonight's major mistake, he was sure that he was going back to the bench for good.

CHAPTER 8

TEAM PLAYERS

Ramon sat quietly in the car as his father drove him to the final practice before the game. With their next to last game coming, the Storm faced a must-win situation against the Murraytown Spiders.

"How's practice been?" asked Ramon's dad.

Ramon was slow to answer. "Okay . . . I guess. Since the last game, the team has helped me learn how to tune out the other team while playing. I also haven't been offsides during transitions all week."

"That all sounds good. Do you know if you're going to start?" his dad asked.

"I don't know, Dad," Ramon said. "I'll find out today."

Ramon looked out the car window to see the entire team standing in the field. They were looking at Ramon as if they'd been waiting for him to arrive.

Ramon's eyebrow rose. "That's odd, I'm normally the early one to practice."

His dad smiled. "Well, don't keep them waiting. And regardless of whether you're starting or not, Mom and I will be in the stands rooting for you and the team."

"Thanks, Dad." Ramon left the car and began to head towards the field and the team. His nerves began to rattle as he got closer. He could see Jax grimacing.

This isn't going to be good, Ramon thought.

Ramon was face-to-face with the entire team. He felt a lump in his throat, but he knew he had to say something. "Hey guys, you're here early. What's up?"

Jax stepped to Ramon, looking him directly in the eyes. "The team had a talk with Coach last night after practice. We told him that we want you to start against Murraytown."

"What?" Ramon was in complete shock. "But, Jax, you can't stand me! Most of you guys have given me a hard time all season."

"After what Bryce said in the locker room, we were wrong for giving you a hard time. All you've done is try to be a team player," said Jax, extending his hand to Ramon. "So, are we cool?"

Ramon shook Jax's hand. "Yeah, we're cool."

The team clapped as Bryce said, "All right everybody, let's get to work! Go Storm!"

CHAPTER 9

A NEW START

Game time. The Centercreek Storm faced a tough challenge on the road against the Murraytown Spiders. Both teams were fighting to make the playoffs. Tonight's winner would be a spot closer to that goal.

Ramon stood on his place on the field, took a deep breath, and waited for the face-off.

Thoughts ran through his head. *Stay focused. Make crisp passes. Don't get distracted. You've got this.*

The opposing team won the face-off. Ramon joined the other midfielders and defenders to stop Murraytown from scoring. Jax was defending his opponent, who was too fast for him. He was so fast that Jax ended up tripping over himself trying to stop him.

"Oof!" said Jax as he fell to the ground.

Ramon saw this and quickly went to cover Jax's opponent before he could take a shot or make a pass. "Switch up and take my guy, Jax!" he said as he covered the player, forcing him to make a bad pass that the Storm stole.

"Go, go, go!" screamed Coach Yen as the Storm transitioned to offense.

The Storm crossed midfield and began passing the ball back and forth as they attempted to find an open shot. Bryce made a bounce pass to Ramon as he ran around causing two Murraytown players to crash into each other.

Ramon passed the ball to Jax, who passed it to another player. That player then passed the ball to an open Bryce, who scored the goal!

The Storm players high-fived each other. "Thanks for picking up for me on defense, Ramon," said Jax.

"No problem," Ramon responded. "Let me stay on the fast guy. You're going to be able to get a bunch of steals if you take my guy."

Jax nodded his head as they prepared for another face-off.

As the game went along, the Storm continued playing great defense and offense. And Ramon had zero offsides penalties!

When the game finally came to an end, the referee blew the whistle as the announcer over the loudspeaker said, "Tonight's final, Centercreek 20, Murraytown 6."

In the locker room, the Storm celebrated. Coach Yen huddled the team together. "Great game tonight," he said. "If we can beat Bracerville next week, we're playoff bound!"

"Let's go Storm! Let's go Storm!" the team yelled in unison.

CHAPTER 10

THE BIG GAME

Ramon sat on the locker room bench with his uniform and gear on. No matter how hard he tried, he could not hide the fact that he was nervous. It was the final game of the regular season, and the pressure was on. He began to take deep breaths and exhaled slowly as Bryce put a hand on his shoulder.

"You okay?" asked Bryce.

"I — I think so," Ramon stuttered. "I've never played in a game this big in my entire life!"

"You're going to be fine," said Bryce. "Let's dig in, back each other up, and do the best we can."

Jax interrupted. "As long as you don't try to tackle the goalie, you'll be fine."

Everybody laughed. It helped break up the nervous energy. A few minutes later the team exited the locker room and ran out onto the field.

The Centercreek stadium was packed! There was not a single empty seat in the stadium.

Wow, Ramon thought. *I've never seen it this crowded before.*

He shook off the nerves as the starting lineup took their positions. His fellow Storm teammates looked at each other and nodded, ready for the battle against the Bracerville Boxers to begin.

The opposing team won the face-off and raced downfield. The midfielders and the defensive players for the Storm were shocked at the speed of Bracerville. Even speedy Ramon was having issues keeping up as the Boxers scored their first goal just minutes into the game!

"These guys are fast!" Ramon yelled.

Jax won the next face-off, and the Storm quickly set up their offense. Again, the speed of Bracerville was making it difficult for Jax, Ramon, Bryce, or anyone else on the offense to make proper passes or get a shot off.

Later in the first half, Coach Yen called for a timeout. The Storm were down 5–3.

"I know you guys need a breather," he said, "badly."

"They're running laps around us!" cried Jax.

"We have to hang in there guys," said Bryce. "There's not much time left in the half, so let's try to get a goal to keep this close. We will find a way to slow them down in the second half. Ramon, set a screen for Jax to free him from his defender. That way I can set him up with a shot at a goal."

"These are big dudes, Ramon. Can you handle it?" asked Jax.

"I've got this," said Ramon.

The Storm took the field as the game started up again. They set up their offense as they brought in the ball. The player defending Jax stuck close to him as Bryce was running with the ball, looking to pass.

Suddenly, Ramon set a screen on the player defending Jax, which set him free. Jax was finally open! Bryce quickly passed to Jax, who then took a shot that passed the Boxers' goalie. The Storm scored!

"Nice screen!" yelled Jax.

"Thanks! I thought your defender was going to run me over!" Ramon joked.

The first-half buzzer sounded and the teams headed off the field. Down by a point, the Storm were going to have to find a way to slow down Bracerville.

* * *

Coach Yen approached his team as players caught their breath and rehydrated during the halftime break. They were exhausted. "That last goal before the half was a great play. Second half, let's run more screens. If they struggle in defending the screen, it gives us more opportunities to score."

The team agreed.

Ramon raised his hand. "Coach, what should we do on defense? We're holding our own the best we can but they wear us down with their speed."

"We're moving to a zone defense for the second half," said Coach. "Playing zone, you guys will be responsible for guarding a specific area on the field. Playing zone will protect our defenders from running everywhere. It will also slow down their offense, and we can make quick double teams on the perimeter and pack the defense in."

"Ramon and I will play the back zones when on defense," said Jax.

* * *

As the second half began, Bracerville won possession of the ball and set up their offense.

Ramon and the others raced to their spots in their defensive zone areas as their goalie yelled, "Sticks up!" This was a reminder to make sure that they close off passing lanes and eliminate bounce passes.

The Storm's zone defense did what it needed to do. The Bracerville players struggled to get a pass or shot off before the shot clock ended, forcing them to turn over the ball.

"It worked!" said Ramon. "The zone worked!"

The Storm took possession of the ball and began to run their offense. Bryce set a screen for Jax, leaving him open for a clean shot. Jax set a screen for Bryce, giving him a clear path to the goal. The screen-led offense was too much for Bracerville as the Storm finally tied the game on a twelve-foot shot from Bryce.

Bracerville continued to get shot-clock violations due to the Storm's great defense. Because Bracerville couldn't get a shot off within a certain period of time, this made them turn over the ball.

However, they finally adjusted to the Storm's screen-based offense, stopping them from taking clear shots on goal and the game was still tied.

With less than a minute left in the game, the Storm continued to attempt to run screens on offense. As Bryce tried to set a screen for Ramon, the opposing player pushed his way through the screen causing him and Bryce to fall to the ground!

The referee blew his whistle. *PHWEET!* "Personal foul," he yelled. "Number nine. Centercreek!"

"That was a bad call, ref!" yelled Coach Yen. "The other player caused the foul by pushing!"

The referee did not agree with the Coach's plea. Due to the time length of the personal foul, Bryce would be out for the rest of the game.

"I'm sorry, guys!" he called as he walked toward the bench. "Do what you can to hold on! You've got this."

Ramon and the others didn't have time to worry as Bracerville attempted to set up a final shot to win the game. But Jax stole a sloppy pass and the Storm raced downfield with seconds on the clock and without their best scorer.

As the Bracerville players surrounded Jax he quickly passed it to Ramon.

Ramon could feel his heart beating through his chest as he ran as fast as he could. With the ball in his stick, he raced closer to the goalie and could feel the goalie's eyes stare him down.

Brushing off defenders, Ramon lifted his stick as if he was going to take a shot. This made the goalie jump to defend the shot, which opened the goal! It was now or never as Ramon took the shot from twenty feet away.

GOAL! GOAL! GOAL! The buzzer sounded as the Storm won the game!

"We did it!" Ramon screamed as his teammates surrounded him and put him on their shoulders. "We're going to the playoffs!"

"Not bad for a sixth grader!" joked Jax.

Ramon laughed as the team celebrated their victory. In the stands, he could see his mother and father cheering and waving at him. For this moment in time, Ramon felt like a legend, and he was going to enjoy this night.

AUTHOR BIO

Shawn Pryor is the creator and cowriter of the all-ages graphic novel mystery series Cash & Carrie, the 2019 GLYPH Nominated football/drama series FORCE, the writer of *Kentucky Kaiju*, and has written multiple titles for Capstone.

GLOSSARY

adjustments (uh-JUST-muhnts)—making necessary changes in order to complete a task

crucial (KROO-shuhl)—something that is of importance

defender (dih-FEN-der)—a player who attempts to stop an opponent from scoring

face-off (FAYS-awf)—when two players try to gain control of the ball

goalie (GOH-lee)—the final line of defense to stop the ball from going into the goal

league (LEEG)—an association of people or groups with common interests or goals

lineup (LINE-up)—a list of players taking part in a game

midfielder (MID-feel-der)—a player in lacrosse that's allowed to play the entire field

offense (AW-fenss)—means of attempting to score

offsides (AWF SIDES)—when one team has more than six players on one half of the field

penalty (PEN-uhl-tee)—a disadvantage put on a team due to not following the rules

position (puh-ZISH-uhn)—the place where a person or thing is or should be

DISCUSSION QUESTIONS

1. Why was Ramon so nervous to switch positions for the eighth-grade team? Do you think his fears or nervousness about making a switch were justified?

2. Why was Jax always so upset with Ramon? Why did he dislike Ramon being on the eighth-grade lacrosse team? Have you ever had a classmate or teammate that you didn't get along with? How did you deal with that person?

3. Bryce was very supportive of Ramon during the lacrosse season. Why? Have you ever played a team sport or been in a scenario where someone else was willing to be supportive or help you? Discuss how that person helped you or someone else on your team at the time.

WRITING PROMPTS

1. This story is told from Ramon's point of view, but there are moments where it can be interesting to see the story from another character's viewpoint. Try rewriting Chapter 5 from Jax's point of view.

2. In Chapter 3, Coach Yen praises Ramon's effort and sees his potential to become a starter for the team. Have you ever had a teacher, coach, or parent who saw potential in you? Write about it.

3. When Ramon scores the winning goal at the end of the game, the team celebrates their victory. Have you ever had a winning moment or something that you could celebrate with your friends?

MORE ABOUT

LACROSSE

American Indians created lacrosse. It was originally called stickball. It was used to bring different tribes and villages together. The activity was also used to condition young men for battle.

The original lacrosse ball was made out of wood. Years later, the ball was made of deer skin and stuffed with fur.

Lacrosse is played in more than 50 countries around the world.

In 1882, the United States began playing lacrosse in boys' high schools.

The year 1904 was the first time that lacrosse was played in the Summer Olympics.

There are two professional lacrosse leagues: Major League Lacrosse, which started in 2001, and the Premier Lacrosse League, which made its debut in 2019.

MORE FROM JAKE MADDOX!

- BLUE LINE BREAKAWAY
- PICK AND ROLL
- DIAMOND DOUBLE PLAY
- UNDERCOVER BMX

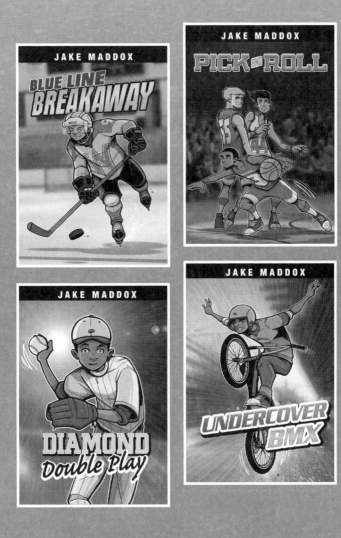

READ THEM ALL !

THE FUN DOESN'T STOP HERE!

DISCOVER MORE JAKE MADDOX BOOKS AT:

capstonepub.com

AND **KEEP**
THE SPORTS
ACTION GOING!